ng starts here!

Every child learns to read in a different way and at his or her own speed. Some go back and forth between reading levels and read favorite books again and again. Others read through each level in order. You can help your young reader improve and become more confident by encouraging his or her own interests and abilities. From books your child reads with you to the first books he or she reads alone, there are I Can Read Books for every stage of reading.

SHARED READING
Basic language, word repetition, and whimsical illustrations, ideal for sharing with your emergent reader

BEGINNING READING
Short sentences, familiar words, and simple concepts for children eager to read on their own

READING WITH HELP
Engaging stories, longer sentences, and language play for developing readers

READING ALONE
Complex plots, challenging vocabulary, and high-interest topics for the independent reader

I Can Read Books have introduced children to the joy of reading since 1957. Featuring award-winning authors and illustrators and a fabulous cast of beloved characters, I Can Read Books set the standard for beginning readers.

A lifetime of discovery begins with the magical words **"I Can Read!"**

Visit www.icanread.com for information
on enriching your child's reading experience.

*For Maya Madelyn, who
loves the farm!*
—A.S.C.

Biscuit and the Little Llamas. Text copyright © 2021 by Alyssa Satin Capucilli. Illustrations copyright ©
2021 by Pat Schories. All rights reserved. Printed in the United States of America. No part of this book
may be used or reproduced in any manner whatsoever without written permission except in the case of brief
quotations embodied in critical articles and reviews. For information address HarperCollins Children's
Books, a division of HarperCollins Publishers, 195 Broadway, New York, NY 10007.
www.icanread.com

Library of Congress Control Number: 2020935524
ISBN 978-0-06-290998-5 (trade bdg.)—ISBN 978-0-06-290997-8 (pbk.)

Typography by Chrisila Maida
20 21 22 23 24 LSCC 10 9 8 7 6 5 4 3 2 1 ❖ First Edition

I Can Read!

Biscuit
and the
Little Llamas

story by ALYSSA SATIN CAPUCILLI
pictures by ROSE MARY BERLIN
in the style of PAT SCHORIES

HARPER
An Imprint of HarperCollinsPublishers

It's a great spring day
on the farm, Biscuit.
Woof, woof!

There's always something new
to see in spring.
Woof, woof!

This way, Biscuit.

Let's see what we can find.

Woof, woof!

Look, Biscuit!

There are the piglets.

Oink! Oink!

Woof!

You found the new colts, too.

Neigh!

Woof!

Funny puppy!

What do you see now?

Woof, woof!

No tugging, Biscuit.
Let's see what else is new
on the farm.
Woof, woof!

Over here, Biscuit.
There are soft lambs
and goats.
Woof, woof!

Oh no, Biscuit.

Not again!

Woof!

Come along now, Biscuit.
There is so much to see
on the farm.

Let's see what else
we can find.
Woof!

Wait, Biscuit!

Come back.

The chicks are over here.

Woof, woof!

Silly puppy!
It's not time to play tug.
Biscuit, let go . . .
Woof!

Oh, Biscuit!
What did you find now?
Woof, woof!

You found a little llama,
Biscuit.
Woof, woof!

Funny puppy!

Another llama found you!

Woof, woof!

You can run and play
with the llamas, Biscuit.
Woof!

You can lead the llamas
to the fresh green grass.
Woof!

You can lead them
to new friends, too.
Woof, woof!

It's fun to see what's new
on the farm in spring, Biscuit.

It's even more fun to find
something new
all by yourself!
Woof! Woof!